~The New Adventures of~
MARY-KATE & ASHLEY™

The Case Of The
HIDDEN HOLIDAY RIDDLE

Look for more great books in

The New Adventures of
MARY-KATE & ASHLEY ™
series:

The Case Of The
HIDDEN HOLIDAY RIDDLE

by Jean Waricha

▥HarperEntertainment
An Imprint of HarperCollins*Publishers*

A PARACHUTE PRESS BOOK

PARACHUTE PRESS

Parachute Publishing, L.L.C.
156 Fifth Avenue
New York, NY 10010

 **DUALSTAR PUBLICATIONS**

Dualstar Publications
1801 Century Park East
12th Floor
Los Angeles, CA 90067

≜HarperEntertainment

An Imprint of HarperCollins*Publishers*
10 East 53rd Street, New York, NY 10022

ISBN 0-06-059594-9

HarperCollins®, ≜®, and HarperEntertainment™ are trademarks of
HarperCollins Publishers Inc.

First printing: November 2004

Printed in the United States of America

www.mary-kateandashley.com

10 9 8 7 6 5 4 3 2 1

THE RIDDLE GAME

"I hope we didn't sleep through breakfast," I said to my sister, Ashley.

Ashley and I were spending Christmas weekend in Washington, D.C., at the home of British Ambassador Jordan. Our Greatgrandma Olive is a friend of Ambassador Jordan, and he had invited the three of us for the holiday.

We hurried down a long, curving staircase. It had a carved golden handrail and really thick red carpeting.

"*I* hope we can find the dining room, Mary-Kate," Ashley said. "This place is huge!"

Ambassador Jordan lived in a big three-story redbrick house. Inside, the house looked like a museum. Portraits of kings and queens in fancy frames lined the walls. Crystal chandeliers hung from the ceilings, and the floors were so shiny, I could see my reflection.

We stopped in the enormous entrance hallway. "Check out the Christmas tree," Ashley said.

"Awesome," I said. The gigantic fir tree was beautifully decorated and lit with tiny white bulbs. Strands of snowy-white popcorn circled the tree. Tiny gift-wrapped packages dangled from the branches, along with gold and silver pinecones. A bright white star glowed at the top of the tree.

"That puts me in the Christmas spirit!" Ashley said.

"My growling stomach puts me in the mood for breakfast," I joked. "Come on."

We entered the dining room. Ambassador Jordan sat at the head of the long table. His grandchildren, Ian and Sarah, sat on either side of him.

Ian was about twelve, with pale skin, red hair, glasses, and lots of freckles. His sister, Sarah, was ten—the same age as Ashley and me. She had her brother's pale skin, but her hair was long, dark, and curly.

"Good morning, girls," Ambassador Jordan greeted us. "Sleep well?" He was a tall, thin man with short blond hair that was turning gray. I figured he was older than our parents but younger than Great-grandma Olive.

"Yes, thank you," Ashley replied. "I love our canopy beds."

Ambassador Jordan had also invited his friends from Wales, Mr. and Mrs. Phelps, and their children, Polly and Marcus, for the weekend. They sat at the other end of the table from the ambassador.

"Sorry we're late," I said, sliding into a chair opposite Polly. Ashley sat down next to me.

Polly was about our age too, with short blond hair and green eyes. Her little blond brother, Marcus, sat beside her.

"Help yourselves to breakfast," said Margaret, the ambassador's housekeeper and cook. She wore a red and green cardigan sweater with gold bells for buttons. She was in the holiday spirit too!

The food on the table looked a lot different from the breakfast I usually ate at home. Where was the cereal? And instead of bagels or waffles I saw plates of fried tomatoes, mushrooms, fried eggs, and some strange, skinny sausages. There was a basket of triangular biscuitlike things, and there were plates of small whole fish, complete from head to tail.

I peeked at Ashley. She looked confused by the food too!

"Why don't you try the kippers?" Mrs. Phelps suggested.

I stared at the table. *Okay, what's a kipper?* I wondered.

Luckily, Ian picked up the plate of fish and handed it to me.

I took a small bite. "That's . . . unusual," I said.

Everyone laughed.

"Here, try a scone," Sarah said. She handed me the basket of biscuitlike things.

"Scones are much like your muffins," Ian explained. "But we don't usually eat them for breakfast."

He had a British accent, but he sounded different from Mrs. Phelps. His accent was more clipped—and kind of snooty.

"I asked Margaret if we could have them for breakfast just this once," Sarah added. "Margaret makes them herself. She even made my favorite kind of scones." She held up her plate. "See? It has chocolate chips."

"That's because you're my special princess," Margaret said, giving Sarah's shoulders a quick squeeze.

Polly rolled her eyes.

I loaded my scone with strawberry jam and took a bite. "Mmm . . . I could get used to this," I said.

"Look what I did," Marcus said.

I glanced at his plate. He had made a smiley face out of his breakfast.

"See, Polly?" He reached to poke her arm to get her attention.

Polly shrank back in her chair. "Don't touch me! You'll get jam all over my dress."

"Marcus, stop bothering your sister," Mr. Phelps said.

Marcus slumped in his chair. He stuck a finger into the jam on his plate and licked it.

"Where's Great-grandma Olive?" I asked, noticing the empty chair.

"Maybe she slept late too," Ashley said.

"Not a chance," Great-grandma Olive said, striding into the room. She wore her long silver hair in a braid, and she had on a thick blue sweater and a pair of slim black jeans. She was carrying a briefcase.

"Do you have work with you, Olive?" Mr. Phelps asked.

"Oh, I worked hard on this, but it was fun." Great-grandma Olive laid the briefcase on the table and patted it.

Ambassador Jordan's blue eyes crinkled into a smile. "Does that mean we're ready to begin?"

"Begin what?" Ashley asked.

I was wondering the same thing.

"I know!" Marcus shouted. "The riddle game."

All the kids at the table looked excited.

"The what?" I asked.

Ambassador Jordan grinned broadly. "Our annual Hidden Holiday Riddle Hunt," he declared. "This year your great-grandma agreed to write the riddles."

"I hid most of the riddles around the house early this morning," she announced. "The first set of riddles are here in my briefcase. I was on my way from the study to my room to drop it off, but I was worried I'd miss breakfast."

"I'd be happy to take the briefcase up to your room," Margaret said, pouring Great-grandma Olive a cup of tea.

"Would you?" Great-grandma Olive asked. "Thank you so much."

As Margaret left the room with our great-grandmother's briefcase, Mr. and Mrs. Phelps excused themselves.

"We have a day of sightseeing planned," Mr. Phelps said.

"I'll walk you out," Ambassador Jordan offered. The three of them left the dining room.

Margaret returned. "There's a phone call

for you," she told Great-grandma Olive.

Great-grandma Olive took a quick sip of tea and then left with Margaret.

"I hope the riddles are harder this year," Ian said. "I need to be challenged."

"Great-grandma Olive is a famous detective," I told the others. "She probably came up with some great riddles."

"I want to win," Marcus whined. He turned to Polly. "You have to help me."

Polly rolled her eyes. "I have better things to do than play some babyish game."

"It's not babyish," Sarah said. "It's fun!"

Ian nodded. "Very mentally stimulating," he said.

I forced myself not to laugh. Ian looked like a normal sixth-grader, but he sounded like an old professor.

"So how does this game work?" Ashley asked.

"It's cool," Sarah said. "Riddles are hidden all over the house. When you solve one riddle, the answer tells you where to find the next one."

"Each time you solve a riddle," Ian added, "you'll find an object. It can be anything—a shoe, a hat, whatever."

"What do you do with the objects?" I asked. "Is it like a scavenger hunt?"

"Sort of," Ian said. "The objects are clues. They help you figure out where in the house the grand prize is hidden."

"Last year Ian and Sarah won free movie passes for a month," Polly grumbled.

"We won the year before that too. And we're going to win again," Sarah said. "Ian is great at solving riddles!"

Ian smiled. He looked a little embarrassed, but I could tell he was really glad that Sarah was bragging about him.

"Well, we're going to give you some competition this year," Ashley said.

"Is that so?" Ian said with a little laugh.

"That's right," I said. "My sister and I are

detectives. We run the Olsen and Olsen Detective Agency out of our attic at home."

"People call us the Trenchcoat Twins," Ashley added with a grin.

"Riddles are our specialty," I declared. I didn't like how Ian was acting—as if he was the only one smart enough to win the game.

"That may be," Ian said. He took off his glasses and wiped them with his napkin. "But you're no match for me! I have studied the cases of Sherlock Holmes, the most famous British detective. In fact, I have my own Holmes detective kit."

"It's not fair!" Marcus complained. "If you two are detectives, and Ian and Sarah always win, I don't have a chance!" He threw down his napkin and rushed out of the room.

Polly sighed. "I'd better go check on him." She pushed her chair away from the table and went in search of her little brother.

Sarah stood up. "I'm done. I'm going to

ask Margaret to make fish-and-chips for lunch." She left the room.

"I was hoping to have sandwiches." Ian sighed. "But Sarah will get her way. Margaret favors her."

"How can you be thinking about lunch already?" I asked, taking a bite of sausage.

Ian shrugged. "And now," he said, standing up, "I'm going to finish reading my latest Sherlock Holmes story. It's great preparation for the Hidden Holiday Riddle Hunt."

He spun around and left the dining room.

I shook my head. "He's a little too sure of himself for me. I don't think he even believes we're detectives."

"He'll find out when the Hidden Holiday Riddle Hunt starts!" Ashley put down her fork and wiped her mouth on her napkin. "Are you done?"

I nodded. "That breakfast was strange but good."

We headed up to our room. As we

strolled along the carpeted hallway, we came to Great-grandma Olive's room. Her door was open.

I looked inside. My mouth dropped open.

Great-grandma Olive was crawling on the floor on her hands and knees!

I grabbed Ashley's arm and dragged her into the room. "Great-grandma Olive, is something wrong?" I asked.

Great-grandma Olive sat back on her heels and looked at us. Her face was flushed and a few strands of hair had come loose from her braid. She pushed the stray hairs out of her face.

"Yes," she said grimly. "Something is very wrong. The first set of riddles that I had in my briefcase are gone. Someone took them!"

2

THE STOLEN RIDDLES

"**G**one?" Ashley gasped. "Are you sure?"

Great-grandma Olive stood up. "The last time I saw them, they were in my briefcase. And now they're not."

"Why would anyone take the riddles?" I asked.

"It's not just the riddle cards," Great-grandma Olive said. "It's the answer sheet for everyone's first riddles too."

Ashley bit her lip. "That means whoever took them got a head start."

"Exactly." Great-grandma Olive's mouth was set in a straight line. "Someone's planning to cheat." She shook her head. "As much as I hate to do this, I'm going to have to cancel this year's Hidden Holiday Riddle Hunt."

Cancel a tradition? That doesn't seem right, I thought. Besides, I wanted to prove to Ian that Ashley and I really were good detectives by winning the challenge.

"Please don't do that," I said.

I could tell Ashley felt the same way I did. "Everyone will be so upset," she said.

"I have an idea," I said. "The best way to find out who took the riddles is to let the game go on. Whoever stole the first riddles and their answers might try to cheat again."

Ashley nodded. "And then we will catch them in the act!"

Great-grandma Olive nodded slowly. "You have a point. And I do hate to disappoint *all* the children because of one person's actions." She smiled. "All right. It looks as if the Olsen and Olsen Detective Agency has a new case."

"And Ashley and I have a game to win!" I said.

"And *I* need to rewrite those first riddles," Great-grandma Olive said.

"Do you remember what the riddles were?" Ashley asked.

"I don't have to." She took a notebook out of the drawer in her nightstand. "I wrote the riddles in this notebook. Then, when I made up my mind which ones to use, I copied them onto the riddle cards."

"While you write out the new cards, we'll start investigating," I said.

"I'm going to get my detective notebook," Ashley said. She hurried to our room down the hall.

Ashley is very organized. She writes down all the clues for our cases in her detective notebook. She never goes anywhere without it, just in case we stumble upon a mystery. Like now!

"Where was the briefcase when you came back to your room?" I asked.

"Right there on the bed," Great-grandma Olive replied.

"Does it have a lock?" I asked.

"Yes, but I didn't bother to use it. I didn't think I needed to." Great-grandma Olive sighed.

Ashley dashed back into the room, gripping her notebook. "Do we have any clues about the riddle thief yet?" she asked.

I was about to answer her when we were startled by a footstep behind us. We all turned around.

Margaret was standing in the open doorway. "Excuse me," she said. "The ambassador has asked everyone to gather in the library to start the Hidden Holiday Riddle Hunt."

Great-grandma Olive smiled at Margaret. "Thank you, Margaret. We'll be right down."

Ashley shut her notebook. "We don't have anything to go on yet," she said. "We'll have to keep our eyes open while we play the game."

We went downstairs. I wondered if we'd really be able to do both—play the game *and* find the riddle thief!

Great-grandma Olive hurried away to rewrite her riddles. Ashley and I stepped into the library. "Wow," I murmured. "There are more books here than in our school library."

Ashley and I plopped down onto the sofa where Polly was sitting. Marcus sat on the floor near the fireplace. Ian strolled into the library, followed by Sarah.

I blinked hard. I couldn't believe what I was seeing.

Ian was wearing a full Sherlock Holmes outfit like I've seen in the movies—a long plaid woolen cape with a matching plaid cap. He carried a large magnifying glass.

"Hey, Ian, it's not Halloween. It's Christmastime," Polly joked.

Ian ignored her. "I'm ready to begin the hunt," he declared. He sounded like an actor in a play.

I caught Polly's eye. We both covered our mouths, trying not to laugh.

Sarah gave her brother a big smile. She obviously thought he looked great.

Great-grandma Olive finally entered the library with Margaret and Ambassador Jordan. She walked to the center of the room, holding the new set of starting riddles.

I looked at Ashley. She was as excited as I was to begin.

Ian seemed very calm. Interesting. I wondered if that was because he already knew the first riddles and their answers!

"We'll start by dividing you into teams," Great-grandma Olive said. "Sarah and Ian, you'll be the Green Team." She handed them a green envelope. "Mary-Kate and

Ashley, you're the Red Team." We were given a red envelope. "Marcus and Polly, you're the Gold Team." They received a gold envelope.

Marcus jumped up and stood by the door as if he was going to race out to start the riddle hunt.

"Remember," Great-grandma Olive continued, "each team has different riddles. They will lead you to different objects. Those objects are clues to where the grand prize is hidden."

This is going to be fun, I thought. *A scavenger hunt with riddles!*

"Let's take our riddle upstairs," I whispered. "Then we can look at it in private."

"Right," Ashley whispered back.

"The contest begins . . . now!" Ambassador Jordan announced. "Good luck, everyone!"

Ian ripped opened his green envelope. Sarah strained to peek at the index card her brother held.

Polly handed Marcus the gold envelope. She looked bored.

"I've got it!" Ian said, snapping his fingers. He raced out of the library. Sarah was right behind him.

"That was quick," I murmured.

"Only if he's actually solved it already," Ashley whispered. "He could be faking to impress everyone."

"Let's go!" I said. Ashley and I dashed up the stairs two at a time. We sat down on the rug in front of the fireplace in our room. My heart pounded as Ashley opened the envelope.

Don't be so nervous, I scolded myself. *There's no way we can lose! We're the Trenchcoat Twins!*

Ashley took out the riddle and read it aloud. "'Riddle Number One. What goes through a door but never comes in or out?'"

"Hmmm . . . This is going to be tougher than I thought," I said.

We sat quietly for a minute, thinking.

"I know!" Ashley shouted, jumping to her feet. "Air!"

I raised one eyebrow. "Air?" I repeated. "Air can't go through a door if it's closed!"

"Oh, yeah." She giggled. "I guess I didn't think it all the way through." She grinned at me. "But at least I came up with an answer. Your turn." She sat back down on the rug.

"All right. What . . . goes . . . through . . ." I dragged out each word. I hoped by the time I finished the sentence, I'd think of an answer.

"Come on. No stalling!" Ashley knew exactly what I was doing. Oh, well. I can't get away with anything with Ashley.

Suddenly we heard a thump outside the bedroom door.

I turned to Ashley and held a finger to my lips. Then I got up, went quietly to the door, and knelt down. I peered through the keyhole.

A brown eye stared back at me!

I gasped. "Someone is spying on us!"

Chapter 3

UNEXPECTED HELP

Ashley yanked open the door.

Marcus tumbled into the room and went sprawling onto the floor.

"Marcus, what are you doing?" Ashley asked as Marcus sat up. "Why were you looking through the keyhole?"

"Uh, I lost something," Marcus mumbled nervously. "I lost, um, a, um, button."

"Marcus," I said, crossing my arms over my chest, "I don't think you're telling the truth. What's really going on?"

Marcus looked as if he was about to cry.

Ashley sat down beside him on the floor. She put an arm around his shoulders. "What's the matter?" she asked.

"I wasn't spying, really. I just . . . I need help solving our riddle," he said. "Polly is too busy talking on the phone. She was mad about coming here this weekend. She wanted to stay home with her friends."

That explained why Polly seemed to be in such a bad mood, I thought.

"Last year I didn't even solve one riddle," Marcus said. "Since you're detectives, I hoped you could help me. Please?" he begged.

"Okay, but just this once," Ashley said. "Hand me your riddle."

I looked at her in surprise.

She shrugged.

Marcus reached for our riddle card on the rug.

"No, that's our riddle," I said. I snatched it up just before he grabbed it.

"Sorry!" Marcus said. He reached into his pocket and took out a crumpled gold envelope. It had jelly stains all over it.

Ashley took the card out of the sticky envelope and read the riddle aloud.

"'What is found in a shell but not in the sea?'" She thought for a minute. "Marcus, I bet you could solve this riddle yourself with a little hint. Want to try?"

A big smile lit up his face. "Sure."

"Okay. What kinds of things have shells?"

His forehead wrinkled. "Polly has a necklace made of shells."

"Those are probably shells that come from the sea," I said. "This is a different kind of shell."

Marcus frowned. "Oh."

"Let's try again," Ashley said. "What comes in a shell and is found in a refrigerator?"

Marcus frowned again. I could see that he was thinking really hard. Then his eyes widened. "Is it . . . an egg?" he asked.

"Yes!" Ashley cheered. "You solved the riddle." She ruffled Marcus's blond hair. "See how smart you are when you try?"

I grinned. Marcus looked very proud of himself. It made me feel good to see him so happy.

"Wow, thanks," Marcus said. "You guys really *are* good!"

He started for the door, then stopped. "Now what do I do?"

"Well, you just solved your first riddle," Ashley explained. "Since the answer to the riddle is an egg, you should look in the refrigerator, where the eggs are kept, to find your next riddle."

"Oh, yeah, I remember now." Marcus nodded. "Thanks."

"You're welcome," I said. I gently pushed him out the door. As cute as he was, we needed to get back the game—*and* our investigation.

Once he was gone, I turned to Ashley.

"Okay, so why did we help him solve his riddle? He's our competition."

"For two reasons," Ashley replied. "One, he looked so sad, and two, he helped solve *our* riddle!"

"What do you mean?" I asked. "How did he do that?"

Ashley grinned. "When you saw him peeking through the keyhole, I figured it out. What goes *through* a door but never comes in or out? A keyhole!"

"Great thinking!" I gave Ashley a high five. We had solved our first riddle!

Then I realized something. Something that made my shoulders sag.

Sure, we'd figured out the riddle. But now we had to find the *right* keyhole—in a house with four hundred rooms!

Okay, maybe not four hundred. But a lot!

"What, exactly, are we looking for?" Ashley asked as we took to the hallways.

I shrugged. "Maybe the next riddle will

be attached somehow to a keyhole or hanging from a doorknob."

Loud voices down the hall caught my attention. "That sounds like Polly and Marcus," I said, "and they're having an argument."

"Do you think it's about the missing riddles?" Ashley asked.

"Let's go see," I said.

We tiptoed down the hallway and stood next to their open door.

"If you don't help me," I heard Marcus say, "I'll tell Mom you took them. Then you'll be in big trouble."

"All right, all right," Polly answered. "I'll help you. But promise you won't tell Mom."

Ashley's blue eyes were huge. "Did you hear what Marcus said?" she whispered. "What do you think he meant?"

"Let's find out," I said. I stepped into the room. Ashley followed me.

"Hey, guys!" I said. "How's it going?"

Polly frowned at me. I wondered if she was worried that Ashley and I had over-heard her argument with Marcus.

"It's going great!" Marcus replied happily. "Polly is going to help me now, because if she doesn't—"

"Marcus!" Polly said sharply.

He looked at his sister. Then he smiled at me and Ashley. "Now maybe *we'll* be the winners."

"We won't have a shot unless we get to work," Polly said. She hurried Marcus out of the room.

I watched them turn the corner at the end of the hall. "We didn't get much infor-mation there," I said.

"Well, we found out that the only reason Polly is playing this game is because Marcus is keeping some sort of secret for her," Ashley said.

"I bet she took those riddles and answers," I said.

"But why?" Ashley asked. "She doesn't really care about the hunt."

"To help out Marcus?" I suggested. "Or maybe she's just pretending that she doesn't care. It did seem to bug her that Ian and Sarah always win."

"That's true," Ashley said. Then she grinned. "And if we don't find the right keyhole soon, Ian and Sarah will win again!"

"Back to keyhole hunting!" I declared.

We rounded a corner and faced another row of rooms. I let out a groan. "I changed my mind about how great this house is," I complained. "It has way too many rooms!"

"Speaking of rooms . . ." Ashley said, peering into a keyhole, "do you think Marcus was putting on an act just to get into our room?"

"Why would he do that?" I asked.

"Polly could have sent him to see what our riddle was. Or to see if we'd solved it."

"He *did* try to grab our riddle card," I said.

"And he *really* wants to win," Ashley added.

"The next room is Great-grandma Olive's," I realized. "Let's stop in to say hello. We can look for clues that might have been left by the riddle thief."

Ashley and I stepped into the room. Great-grandma Olive wasn't there.

"Do you think she'll mind if we just take a quick look around?" I asked, peering behind the door.

"I don't think we should—" Ashley started to say. She stopped and stared at something sticking out from under the bed.

My eyes widened as I watched her bend down . . . and then wriggle under the bed!

"What are you doing?" I asked.

Ashley wriggled back out, holding something in her hands.

"Mary-Kate, look what I found!" she said as she sat up. "The missing riddles!"

4

IN THE PINK

I stared at the red, green, and gold envelopes in my sister's hand. "The riddles! What were they doing under the bed?"

"I don't know," Ashley replied.

"Maybe the riddle thief tried to return them to Great-grandma Olive's briefcase but couldn't find it," I said.

"And maybe they were afraid of getting caught with the riddles, so they just threw them under the bed," Ashley added. She handed me the envelopes.

I examined the three green, gold and red envelopes. "Do you see these pinkish smudges?" I pointed to smears on the envelopes.

"Evidence!" Ashley cried. "The person who took the riddles must have made these smudges. Great-grandma Olive would never give out envelopes with smudges on them."

"You're right," I agreed. "She's much too neat."

Ashley took the envelopes back from me and studied them closely. "You know, that pink stuff could be the strawberry jam we had with breakfast this morning."

"Marcus was covered with jam this morning, remember?" I leaned in to take a whiff. "Hmm . . . it does smell fruity."

Ashley pulled her detective notebook out of her pocket and opened it to a clean page. At the top of the page she wrote: *Suspects*. She hesitated.

"I don't know, Mary-Kate," she said. "I

realize Marcus *could* be a suspect, but it's hard to believe. He is only six, after all."

"True," I replied. "But remember, we have to consider everyone. And so far he's our best candidate."

Ashley wrote *Marcus* as the first name on the suspect list. Then she wrapped the envelopes in a tissue and slipped them into her pocket.

"You know," Ashley said, "whoever stole these cards still has the answers to the first riddles."

"That might get Marcus off the suspect list," I said. "If he had the answers, why would he have needed our help?"

"Unless he was faking it," Ashley suggested. "Maybe what he really wanted was to slow us down while Polly went and got their next riddle."

"Possible," I said. "We should get back to the game. Finding these missing riddle cards slowed us down too."

"And we still have a keyhole to find!"

Ashley and I dashed out the door and nearly ran over Polly and Marcus.

Uh-oh. Did they overhear us discussing them as suspects? I wondered.

"Hi, guys. Find anything yet?" Polly asked. Her smile looked kind of phony.

"We're working on it," Ashley answered.

Marcus grinned. "Polly said we're going to win this year," he said.

"Come on, Marcus," ordered Polly. "If you want to win this silly game, you've got to keep up."

Polly took off down the hall with Marcus at her heels.

"Did you notice something different about her?" Ashley asked.

"I think she was wearing lipstick," I said. "*Pink* lipstick! And it looks like it could be a match for the smudges on the envelopes!"

Ashley pulled out her detective notebook and wrote Polly's name under

Marcus's. She tapped the page with her pencil. "But how would Polly's lipstick get onto the envelopes?"

I giggled. "I doubt she kissed them!"

Ashley laughed.

"She could have used the kind of lipstick that comes in little pots," I said. "You use your fingers for that."

"What are you writing?"

The voice behind us startled me. I whirled around and saw Sarah.

"Wow," I said. "I didn't hear you coming."

Sarah laughed. "That's why these thick carpets are great," she said. "I can sneak out of bed and get a snack, and no one will hear me!"

Ian strolled around the corner. He still wore his Sherlock Holmes outfit.

And it still made me want to crack up! I bit the insides of my cheeks to keep from laughing.

"How's the hunt going?" Ashley asked.

"We've already solved two riddles, and we have our first clue to the grand prize!" Sarah said.

"That was fast," remarked Ashley.

"We're a good team," Sarah said. She smiled up at Ian. "Isn't that right, Ian?"

"True. You've definitely improved this year. You figured out that first riddle quite well."

Sarah blushed. I could see she really looked up to her older brother.

"You may as well give up now," Ian told us. "You're no match for me. I even belong to a detective club at school."

"He wants to be president of the club next year," Sarah confided.

"Come on, Sarah. Let's go to the kitchen for a much-deserved beverage," Ian said, striding down the hall.

"Can't he just say 'I'm getting a drink' like a normal person?" I muttered.

Sarah lingered behind. I was surprised

she wasn't following Ian like a puppy.

"My brother always wins," she bragged. "And with my help . . ."

I was getting tired of Sarah's telling us how her brother always won. We weren't giving up so easily.

"Well, of course you always win," I said. "This is the first time we've ever been in this house, so it takes us twice as long as you to find things."

Sarah bit her lower lip, considering this. "You're right," she decided. "I want us to beat you two fair and square. Maybe I can help you find what you're looking for now."

I was surprised. "Thanks." It was cool that she was willing to help us, even though we were her biggest competition.

"The answer to our riddle is a keyhole," Ashley said. "But there must be dozens of keyholes in this house. Is one of them somehow different?"

Sarah's face scrunched up in thought.

"Well—there's a really big keyhole in the attic door. It's antique or something. That could be it. Follow me!"

We climbed up a set of stairs, then down a long hallway and up a dark, narrow staircase. We stopped at an old wooden door with big black hinges. Beneath the doorknob was a shiny black keyhole! It was round at the top and square at the bottom, and it was large enough for a mouse to fit through it. I didn't really want to think about mice in the attic, though. They give me the creeps.

"Here it is. Well, good luck," Sarah said. Then she ran down the stairs to find her brother.

Ashley peeked through the keyhole.

"It's there!" she said. "I think I see a red envelope on the floor. Our first clue to the prize must be in there!"

"What are we waiting for?" I said.

Ashley tugged at the doorknob, but the door didn't open.

"Let me try," I said.

I grabbed the doorknob with both hands and pulled as hard as I could. No luck. Finally, with both of us pulling, the door swung open, nearly knocking us over. Cautiously we stepped inside the attic.

"Whoa!" I yelped, tripping over a box. "It's too dark in here."

"Let's let our eyes adjust for a second," Ashley said.

The attic had a dusty, musty smell that made me want to sneeze. A small window let in a little light from across the room.

Wooden crates and cardboard boxes were stacked against the walls. Old trophies, photo albums, a high chair, and some sports equipment lay scattered around us.

Ashley and I stared at the red envelope on the floor across the room. "Go get it!" Ashley said.

"Me?" I said, staring at her. "Why me?"

To get that envelope I would have to walk

through a maze of cobwebs hanging from the low ceiling. No way. I hated cobwebs.

"All right," Ashley said. "We'll both go."

Ashley and I held hands and crept forward. Ashley grabbed an old sweater from an open box to use to brush away the cobwebs. She dropped it fast when moths fluttered up from the sweater!

We shrieked and ran for the envelope.

"I got it!" I shouted. "Let's get out of here!"

A loud slam behind us made me jump. We whirled around.

"It was just the door," Ashley said in a shaky voice.

We crossed the room and Ashley tried to open the door.

"It's stuck," Ashley said, tugging on the doorknob.

I set down the envelope on the floor and the two of us tried to open the door, but it wouldn't budge.

"We're trapped!" Ashley cried.

5

TRAPPED!

We tugged on the doorknob harder. And harder. We put our hands flat against the door and pushed with all our weight. It wouldn't budge an inch.

"It's really stuck," Ashley said miserably.

"Okay, stay calm," I said, even though the attic gave me the shivers. "There's got to be a light switch around here somewhere."

Ashley felt along the wall for a switch. "Here it is," she said, flipping a switch. Dim light filled the room from a single bare bulb in the ceiling.

I was sure I heard the sound of mice scampering away from the light.

We searched the attic for another way out. There was only the one small window, high up in the wall.

"Let's try the door again," Ashley suggested. Together we hit the door, smashed into it, and even kicked it. No luck.

"Time out," I said, sitting down on a trunk. I stared at the door, *wishing* it would open. That didn't work either!

"Hey, look at this," Ashley said. She pointed to some pink marks on the door. "Those look like fingerprints to me," she said.

"And they look just like the smudges on the stolen riddles," I said.

Ashley pulled out the envelopes we'd found under Great-grandma Olive's bed. She held them up next to the marks on the attic door.

"The smudges are the same!" she said.

My heart pounded with excitement. This was real evidence.

"That means that whoever stole the riddles from Great-grandma Olive's room also touched the attic door," I declared. "But why?"

"I don't know," Ashley said as she rattled the doorknob again. I could see she was really frustrated. "What I do know is that we need to get out of here!"

We began pounding and yelling together. "Help! Anyone out there? We're stuck in the attic!"

We waited, but no one came.

"There must be some other way out. We can't just sit here and wait to be rescued," I told Ashley.

We looked around the attic. Nothing there but boxes and old things.

"I have an idea. If we stack up some of these crates, maybe we can reach that window. Then we can see if there's any way to climb down to the ground," Ashley suggested.

We worked in silence for a few minutes, pushing and pulling and lifting crates. Ashley pulled herself up, stood on tiptoe, and peeked out the window.

"There's no way to climb down here," she said.

"Can you open the window and call for help?" I asked.

Ashley pushed open the window. "Hey, down there!" she yelled. "Anybody! We're stuck in the attic!" She paused, then whistled her loudest whistle.

I climbed up beside her and looked down. She whistled again.

Two large German shepherds raced around a corner of the house, barking loudly.

"Well, *somebody* heard us," I told Ashley.

Now two security guards dashed after the dogs.

"Up here!" I shouted as loudly as I could. I had to drown out those dogs. They were making a real racket!

Both guards looked up. "Are you all right?" one of them called out to us.

"We're fine, but the attic door is stuck," Ashley shouted.

"Stay put. I'll be right up!" shouted the other guard.

"As if we could go anywhere anyway," Ashley said, laughing, as we carefully climbed back down to the floor.

We waited for what seemed like hours, but I'm sure it was only a few minutes. The guard jiggled the door and rattled the knob.

Finally the door swung open.

"You girls should know better than to play up here," said the guard as he swung the creaky door open. "It's a good thing Tea and Crumpet heard you yelling."

"Who?" Ashley and I asked together.

"The German shepherds," he explained.

Then he gave us a curious look. "How did this door get locked anyway?"

Ashley and I glanced at each other. "What do you mean, 'locked'?" I asked. "We thought the door just got stuck."

"This door was locked from the outside," the guard explained. "Someone must have turned this little knob." He demonstrated how the lock worked. "Whoever locked this door must not have realized you girls were in the attic."

Or, I thought, *someone locked us in the attic on purpose!*

6

A STRANGE CLUE

Ashley and I hurried back to our room to discuss the case.

"Okay," Ashley said, taking out her detective notebook. "Who would lock us in the attic—and why?"

"It's obvious," I said. "The person who locked us in the attic doesn't want us to win the game!" I paused. "Sarah brought us to the attic. . . . Do you think she's the one who locked us in?"

"She's definitely a suspect now," Ashley

said. She wrote Sarah's name on the list.

"Wait a second," I said. "Whoever took the riddles and answer sheet *knew* that our first riddle would send us to the attic. It could have been anyone!"

Ashley groaned and looked at her notebook. "The only person *not* on this list is Ian."

"Yet," I said.

"Okay, let's start at the beginning. Who had the chance to take the starting riddles?" Ashley said.

I thought back to breakfast. "Great-grandma Olive told us that the riddles were in her briefcase," I said. "Then everyone heard Margaret offer to take the briefcase up to her bedroom."

"That's right," Ashley said. "And all of our suspects left the breakfast table before we did."

"So they all could have had time to get to her room and take the riddles," I said.

Ashley chewed on the end of her pencil.

"Let's talk about motives," she suggested. "*Why* would someone steal the riddles?"

I shrugged. "Everyone wants to win."

"But who wants to win so much, they would cheat?"

"Marcus wants to win really badly, and Polly is helping him so he'll keep some kind of secret for her," I said. "So that could be a motive for both of them."

"Ian really wants to win to keep his perfect record," Ashley pointed out.

"And Sarah wants to do anything Ian wants to do," I said.

"They *will* win if we're too busy chasing the riddle thief," I pointed out. "Let's solve the new riddle, and then we'll concentrate on finding the thief again."

Ashley nodded. "You're right. Let's see what our first clue to the grand prize is."

I opened the red envelope.

"Huh?" I pulled a pine-scented air freshener out of the envelope. The kind that dangles from a car's rearview mirror. I held it up to show Ashley.

"Ohhh-kay," she said, taking the miniature cardboard tree from me. She stared at it a minute, then slipped it into her detective notebook.

"That's a little strange," I said. "Do you think it means that the grand prize is a car?" I laughed.

"It doesn't mean anything right now," Ashley said. "When we find all our other clues, it should make sense."

"I hope so," I said. "Because right now, that's just plain weird."

"And now for the riddle," Ashley announced. She pulled the riddle card out of the same envelope.

"'Riddle Number Two: What animal is most like a tree?'" she read out loud. She looked at me. "Any ideas?"

"Well . . . an elephant is like a tree," I said. "Both have trunks."

"True," said Ashley. "But have you noticed any elephants around here?"

I giggled. "That would be funny!"

We sat down on the rug and tossed around ideas. Frogs, because they're green? Giraffes, because they're tall?

I jumped up to my feet. "I've got it!" I shouted. "A dog is most like a tree—they both have 'bark'!"

Ashley's eyes lit up. "Yes! You did it!" she cheered. Then her face fell.

"What's wrong?" I asked.

"The only dogs we've seen here are those big, growling German shepherds," Ashley said.

I shrugged. "So?"

Ashley gulped. "Well, if a dog is the answer to the riddle, that means our next riddle card and clue will be on or with one of those scary dogs."

7

NICE DOGGIE?

Would Great-grandma Olive really make us visit the big scary dogs? I wondered.

"Maybe it's not *on* the dogs exactly," I said. "Maybe the riddle is hidden in their doghouse."

Ashley looked relieved. "That does make sense," she agreed. "Tea and Crumpet can't be in their doghouse all the time."

"Even if they are in the doghouse, Great-grandma Olive would never put us in danger," I reasoned.

"Maybe the dogs are friendlier than they look," Ashley said, sounding hopeful.

"How bad could they be with cute names like Tea and Crumpet, right?" Just saying this made me feel better.

Ashley nodded.

We went through the kitchen to get to the back door. Margaret was in the kitchen frosting cookies. She wore a red and green apron over her black and white uniform.

The kitchen was very warm from all her baking and cooking. *No wonder she took off her holiday sweater*, I thought.

"Care for some cookies, girls?" she asked, holding out a plate.

"Sure," Ashley said, grabbing two.

I didn't take any. I was too nervous to eat.

We stepped onto the wooden porch and stopped. We both stared at the huge white doghouse.

"Okay, come on," I said. "If we don't go now, we never will."

We took two baby steps toward the dog-house. So far, so good. There were no signs that read: BEWARE KILLER DOGS.

We took another two baby steps. The big dogs were fast asleep inside the doghouse.

"See? They're really cute," Ashley said.

"That's because they're sleeping," I whispered.

We tiptoed closer. "Nice doggies," Ashley whispered. "Don't wake up for us."

Ashley was right. They did look cute. They even reminded me of Clue, our own sweet basset hound at home. Maybe they weren't so scary after all.

"Here goes," Ashley whispered. She ducked down to enter the doggie door. "I don't see any red envelope." She kept her voice low.

I crawled in after her.

That's when Ashley straightened up and banged her head on the doghouse roof.

"Ouch!" she yelped.

Tea and Crumpet opened their eyes and stared at us. We stared at Tea and Crumpet. For a moment no one moved.

Then Crumpet began to growl, a low, rumbling sound. Tea snarled.

"Good doggie!" Ashley said softly. "Want a cookie?"

The two dogs sprang to their feet.

I froze. I remembered reading that you should slowly back away from an angry dog.

"Stay calm," I whispered to Ashley as we inched back. My heart was beating so loudly, I was sure that Ashley and the dogs could hear it.

Ashley threw her two cookies at the dogs. Yes! The dogs stopped to munch on the cookies—and we ran!

With loud barks, the dogs lunged for us. But they suddenly stopped in their tracks.

"They're on chains!" Ashley shouted. "That's as far as they can go!"

"Phew!" I collapsed onto the ground.

Ashley dropped down beside me. "That was some narrow escape!" she panted.

"That's for sure," I agreed, waiting for my heart to slow back down to normal.

I lay on the cold ground, thinking. Something just wasn't right. Great-grandma Olive would never have put us in danger. I took out the riddle card and read it again.

"Ashley! Why didn't we notice this before?" I cried out. "This riddle is written in pink ink, not in black like the others. And it's the same color pink as the smudges on the stolen riddles and on the attic door!"

Ashley's eyes widened. "That means Great-grandma Olive didn't write this riddle," she said. "Someone else did! This riddle is a fake!"

8

A FAKE!

We got up off the ground and brushed the dirt from our clothes. Ashley took out her notebook.

Under *Evidence*, she wrote: *Phony riddle written in pink ink matches smudges on stolen riddles and on attic door.*

We walked back to the house slowly, deep in thought.

"This is a really important clue in the case," Ashley said. "This means that the same person who stole the starting riddles also locked us in the attic *and* switched our riddle cards."

"If we can find the owner of the pink pen," I added, "we'll find our cheater!"

We opened the back door and went into the kitchen. Margaret stood at the stove, stirring a big pot of soup.

"We're having homemade tomato soup and grilled cheese sandwiches for lunch," Margaret said. "I trust you girls enjoy those."

"Oh, yes," I said.

"I guess Sarah didn't get her way this time," Ashley commented.

"What do you mean?" Margaret asked.

"Oh, after breakfast Sarah said that she was going to the kitchen to ask you to make fish-and-chips for lunch today," Ashley explained.

Margaret frowned. "If she'd asked me, I certainly would have made that for her. The little love."

I raised my eyebrows at Ashley. Margaret

really did play favorites. And Sarah was it.

We left the kitchen. "If Sarah didn't go to the kitchen after breakfast," Ashley said, "she might have had time to go to Great-grandma Olive's room and steal the riddles."

"So, where to?" I asked. "We can try to find our real riddle, or we can try to solve this case."

"Let's question our suspects," Ashley suggested.

As we passed the front door, we heard a loud crash inside the hall closet.

Ashley and I stared at each other. What could have made that noise?

We approached the door slowly and carefully. I pulled it open to find . . . Marcus. He lay on the closet floor in a tangle of coats.

"Marcus? What are you doing in there?" Ashley asked, helping him up.

"I was looking for this," he said, holding up an umbrella. He stepped out of the closet.

"It's not raining, Marcus," I said. "Why do you need an umbrella?"

Marcus pulled an index card out of his pocket. "It's the answer to my riddle!"

I took the riddle and read it aloud. "'What can go up a chimney when it's down but can't come down a chimney when it's up?'"

I handed the riddle back to him. "That's a tough one. How did you figure it out?"

"Polly told me the answer," he admitted. "She said a closed umbrella is an umbrella that's 'down.' And it can fit *up a* chimney . . ."

"I get it," Ashley said. "But an open umbrella—an umbrella that's 'up'—can't come down a chimney."

"Yup!" Marcus nodded happily. "Polly *had* to help me. I told her I'd tell on her if she didn't!"

"Tell on her about what, Marcus?" I asked.

Marcus took a step back. "Nothing," he said quickly. He pulled a gold envelope out of the folds of the umbrella. "And look, here's my next riddle *and* my clue to the big prize." He ran off, waving the gold envelope.

"He left a mess in here," Ashley said. She picked up a red and green cardigan sweater with gold bells for buttons. A red riddle card fell out of the pocket.

Ashley grabbed it. "This is our missing riddle card!" she gasped. "It says 'Number Two' right up on top. What's it doing here?"

I stared at the cardigan. "I know that sweater. Margaret was wearing it at breakfast!"

Ashley's eyes widened. "Do you think Margaret stole the riddles?" she asked.

I thought about it. "Well, she had the opportunity," I said. "Margaret was the one who took Great-grandma's briefcase with the riddles in it upstairs."

Ashley nodded. "And Margaret does love Sarah," she said. "Her motive could be that she wanted to help Sarah win."

"Let's go find Margaret. We need to ask her a few questions," I said, heading back to the kitchen.

Ashley followed behind me. "Hello? Anyone here?" she called.

No answer.

Just then I spotted a note on the table. It was a grocery list: *flour, chocolate chips, baking soda.*

The note was written in pink ink.

"Ashley," I said, picking up the note, "take a look at this."

I handed her the grocery list. Her eyes widened when she saw the pink writing. She pulled the fake riddle out of her pocket.

"It's the same color and the same handwriting," she said.

"Which means Margaret must be the riddle thief!" I added.

9

AND THE WINNER IS . . . ?

Before we could move, we heard Sarah's excited voice coming from the library, next to the front hall. "We won! We won!" she shouted.

Ashley and I ran to the library. We found Sarah jumping up and down. Ian stood beside her, beaming.

Mr. and Mrs. Phelps, Great-grandma Olive, and Ambassador Jordan were all in the library too.

Margaret entered right behind us.

"What's all the ruckus about?" she asked.

"We solved all three of our riddles and found all our grand prize clues," bragged Ian. He held up a bag.

"You haven't won yet," Polly pointed out sourly, as she and Marcus entered the room. "You still haven't found the grand prize."

Polly's mother looked at her. "Don't be disappointed, dear." Then she frowned. "Polly, are you wearing lipstick?" she asked.

Polly ran a hand through her blond hair. She seemed nervous.

"And is that nail polish?" Mrs. Phelps asked. "Where did you get lipstick and nail polish?"

"She took them from your dresser!" Marcus blurted out.

"Marcus!" Polly said, flushing deep pink. "You promised not to tell," she whispered furiously. Then she looked up at her mother.

"I only *borrowed* your lipstick and nail polish. I didn't *take* them."

"Polly, what did I say about wearing makeup?" her mother said. "And about taking my things?"

"I know," Polly mumbled.

Ashley and I looked at each other. So that's what Polly's big secret was! She took her mom's makeup.

Sarah walked up to us with a smug expression. "I guess the Trenchcoat Twins aren't so great after all." She turned to Ian. "Maybe I can be in your detective club now too," she said eagerly.

"You did do rather well," Ian said. "Especially with our first riddle. You surprised me."

"Congratulations, Sarah," I said cheerfully. "We should celebrate with your favorite lunch today. . . . Oh, but it's too bad we're not having fish-and-chips."

"What?" Sarah looked confused.

"After breakfast you said you were going to the kitchen to find Margaret. You were going to ask her to make fish-and-chips for lunch," I reminded her. "But you didn't go to the kitchen, did you?"

"No, she didn't," Margaret agreed. "I was there. I would have been happy to make her favorite lunch if she'd asked."

Exactly.

"Well, Sarah," Ashley said, catching on, "at least you'll be able to have your favorite scones tomorrow. Chocolate chips are on Margaret's grocery list."

Margaret looked confused. "I didn't write a grocery list."

"Oh, I did it," said Sarah. She smiled at Margaret. "I was just trying to help."

That clinched it. I looked at Ashley, and she nodded. She got it too.

"We saw the list on the kitchen table," I told Sarah. "It was written in pink. That's a great color. But the pen leaks, doesn't it?"

"Yeah," Sarah said. "How did you know that?"

Ashley reached for Sarah's hand. She held it up to show everyone the pink smudges on Sarah's fingers.

"The ink smells nice too, I bet," I said.

"That's why I like it. It's called Tutti-Frutti." Sarah giggled nervously. She was a lot less sure of herself now.

I could tell she was wondering why we were talking so much about her pen.

Ashley took the fake riddle from her pocket—the one we found in the attic, that sent us to the doghouse.

She held it up in front of Sarah.

"What—what's that?" Sarah stammered.

"Don't you recognize it?" Ashley asked her. "It's the fake riddle that someone left for us."

I took out the grocery list Sarah had written and held it next to the riddle in Ashley's hand.

"Sarah, the ink and the handwriting are the same as on the grocery list you wrote," I declared. "You wrote this fake riddle, didn't you?"

Sarah's eyes widened. She knew she was caught. "I . . . but . . . that's just . . ."

Ambassador Jordan stepped over to his granddaughter. "What's going on, Sarah?" he asked, placing a hand on her shoulder. "Did you cheat to win the Hidden Holiday Riddle Hunt?"

10

THE FINAL CLUES

The room fell silent, and all eyes turned toward Sarah.

"I didn't do anything that bad!" she said.

I glanced at Ian. He just looked confused.

"I just wanted our team to win," she said. "Ian is a really smart detective, but I wasn't sure he could beat the Trenchcoat Twins. I thought I could help. And then he'd see that I was a good detective too. He might even let me join his detective club."

Ambassador Jordan looked troubled. "Cheating isn't the same as 'helping,'" he said. "Sarah, did you steal the starting riddles and the answer sheet from Olive's briefcase?"

Sarah looked down at her shoes. "Yes," she confessed. "I went to Olive's room after breakfast to ask her for advice. She wasn't there, but I saw her briefcase, and I knew the riddles were inside. I was going to peek at them and put them back, but I heard someone coming."

She looked up and started talking fast to get it all out quickly. "I shoved the riddles and answers into my pocket and read them in my room. When I went to put them back, I didn't see the briefcase, so I tossed them under the bed."

"You knew the answer to our first riddle was the attic keyhole, right?" I asked. "So you went up to the attic *before* you led us there, and you switched the riddle cards."

Sarah nodded miserably.

"And then you locked us in the attic to slow us down, didn't you?" Ashley asked.

"Yes," she mumbled.

"Sarah, why did you use a fake riddle to send us to the doghouse?" I asked.

Ambassador Jordan looked shocked. "You sent Mary-Kate and Ashley to our security doghouse?" he demanded.

"I didn't think anything bad would happen to them," Sarah explained. "Tea and Crumpet are always nice to me."

"They've known you since you were a baby," Ambassador Jordan pointed out. "Mary-Kate and Ashley are strangers to them."

"Oh," Sarah said in a small voice. "I'm sorry. I didn't mean any harm. I swear. I just wanted to slow them down even more."

"You hid our real riddle in Margaret's sweater, didn't you?" I asked.

Sarah nodded. "I had to get rid of your real riddle card. Margaret's sweater was hanging on a chair in the kitchen, and she wasn't around, so I slipped it into a pocket. I was going to go back to get it—"

This time Margaret interrupted Sarah. "But I'd hung it in the hall closet."

"Which is where we found it," Ashley finished up.

"This is very disappointing," Great-grandma Olive said. "Your grandfather and I worked very hard to plan this riddle hunt."

"I know," Sarah said. "I'm sorry. Can't everyone else finish the game without me?"

"I don't see how," answered the ambassador. "Your team had a big head start, and Mary-Kate and Ashley never had a fair chance to compete."

Ian stepped forward. "Why don't I show everyone *our* clues to the grand prize? Then we'll all have an equal chance to find it."

That seemed fair to me. I looked at Great-grandma Olive and Ambassador Jordan. They whispered together a minute.

"All right," Ambassador Jordan said. "But, Sarah, I'll have a list of extra chores for you when we're done."

Sarah just nodded.

Ian sat on the floor and took his clues out of the bag. Everyone crowded around him.

"Scotch tape," he said, pulling the dispenser out of his bag. "Popcorn. Pinecone."

Ashley looked at me. "We found an air freshener," she said. She pulled it out of her detective notebook and set it next to the other objects.

"We found two clues," Marcus piped up.

Polly pulled out a tiny light bulb and a piece of shiny ribbon from two gold-colored envelopes.

Everyone stared at the pile of objects. The clues had us all stumped.

Ashley began to think out loud. "What do these objects have in common?"

Marcus sat down in front of all the objects. "Tape is sticky," he said. "So are pinecones sometimes. And so is popcorn!"

"Only because you like caramel popcorn," Polly said. "Plain popcorn isn't sticky."

"Is there someplace we might find all these things together?" I suggested.

"A store!" Marcus said. "You could buy all these things in a store."

Ashley shook her head. "The grand prize is *here* somewhere," she said. "And you find pinecones on pine trees, not at a store."

Pine trees, I thought. My brain started clicking.

I went to the large double doors leading to the entrance hallway and pulled them open. The tiny white lights on the Christmas tree sparkled. The popcorn strands and fancy little gift boxes stood out against the deep green pine needles.

"Pinecone and pine-scented air freshener for the pine tree," I said.

Ashley dashed over to stand beside me. "Popcorn for the popcorn strands!"

"A lightbulb for the Christmas lights!" I said.

"And Scotch tape and ribbon to wrap the gifts!" Ashley added.

"It's the Christmas tree!" we both shouted together.

We whirled around to look at the others. Great-grandma Olive beamed, and Ambassador Jordan nodded. Even Ian looked impressed.

"Let's go find the prize!" Marcus said.

We all raced over to the tree. Everyone searched the prickly branches.

"I've got it!" Ashley cried.

She pulled a red, green, and gold envelope from the lower branches. Inside was a cream-colored card with fancy gold writing on it.

"Wow!" I gasped. "This is an invitation to the White House for their big Christmas party!"

We threw our arms around Great-grandma Olive.

"Thank you!" I said.

"We get to meet the president of the United States!" Ashley said. "What a great prize!"

"And what great detective work," Great-grandma Olive told us.

"You're really lucky," Marcus said.

"That party is going to be seriously cool," Polly agreed. "I bet there will be famous people there and TV cameras and everything."

"Great job, you two," said Ian.

Ashley and I looked at each other. I knew she was thinking the same thing.

I turned to Ambassador Jordan and

Great-grandma Olive. "I know Ashley and I were the ones who figured out the grand prize," I said. "But we all shared our clues. Is there any way we could all go to the party?"

Great-grandma Olive looked even happier than when we'd solved the mystery. "What a lovely idea," she said.

"I'll arrange invitations for everyone," Ambassador Jordan said.

"I have to admit, you two are excellent detectives," Ian said. "Perhaps you'd like to be honorary members of my detective club."

Wow. I never thought I'd hear such high praise from Ian.

Ashley smiled. "Will we have to dress like Sherlock Holmes?" she asked.

Ian grinned back. "It isn't a requirement."

"In that case," she said, "we accept!"

Hi from both of us,

Ashley and I were spending the week at the Icy Igloo Inn. The inn is made totally out of ice . . . the walls, the furniture, even the beds! But then we discovered that some ice vases had melted, and a chair and table were dripping. Oh, no! More and more things were starting to melt! It was too cold in the hotel for anything to melt on its own. Someone was melting the Icy Igloo Inn!

Could we crack this case before the Inn melted away? Want to know what happened? Turn the page for a sneak peek at *The New Adventures of Mary-Kate and Ashley: The Case Of The Icy Igloo Inn.*

See you next time!

Mary-Kate Olsen   *Ashley Olsen*

The New Adventures of
MARY-KATE & ASHLEY ™

A sneak peek at our next mystery…

The Case Of The
ICY IGLOO INN

Ashley and I still couldn't believe it. It was winter break and we were staying in a hotel made totally out of *ice*! The walls were made out of ice. All of the furniture was carved out of ice too. Luckily the floors were made of hard-packed snow so we didn't need ice skates!

It was dinnertime and we all sat at a dining room table carved out of ice. The owners, Iris and Irving, served us cold chicken and pasta salad.

"Look!" Ashley nodded at her dish. "Even the plates here are made out of ice."

"Cold plates, cold food," Dakota complained. "I wish we could have a hot meal!"

I looked at Kevin to see how he was enjoying the meal. Then I saw something weird. Kevin's plate looked soggy and wet—as if it was melting!

That's funny, I thought. *No one else's plate is melting.*

"Oh, dear!" Iris's voice interrupted my thoughts. "I forgot to decorate our dinner table with my ice vases. They're still in the living room."

"I saw your vases," Lars said. "All those great shapes and sizes. They are awesome."

"I'd love to see them," I said.

"Sure," Irving said. "Let's go." He cracked a little smile. "It's not like your dinner will get cold!"

Ashley and I followed Iris and Irving into the living room. Iris let out a huge gasp.

"My ice vases!" she cried. "They're gone!"

Iris pointed to a table made out of ice. There were bunches of dried flowers on the table. And puddles of water that seemed to have frozen!

"I hate to tell you this, Iris," Ashley said. "But I think your vases melted."

That's what I thought too.

"Melted?" Iris and Irving cried.

"Impossible!" Irving said. He walked over to a thermometer hanging on the wall. "It's twenty-five degrees in here. Nothing in the Icy Igloo Inn ever melts in twenty-five degrees!"

Ashley looked around. "And look—nothing else in this room melted."

"So what are you saying?" Iris asked.

"This was no accident," I said. "Someone melted your ice vases on purpose!"

Mary-Kate and Ashley

Win an "Apple iPod®" Sweepstakes

A PORTABLE DIGITAL MUSIC PLAYER!

Record hours of music from your favorite CDs or online music sites! Load it up and carry it in your pocket!

The New Adventures of Mary-Kate and Ashley
Apple iPod® Sweepstakes
OFFICIAL RULES:

1. **NO PURCHASE OR PAYMENT NECESSARY TO ENTER OR WIN.**

2. **How to Enter.** To enter, complete the official entry form or hand print your name, address, age and phone number along with the words "New Adventures Apple iPod® Sweepstakes" on a 3" x 5" card and mail to: New Adventures Apple iPod® Sweepstakes, c/o HarperEntertainment, Attn: Children's Marketing Department, 10 East 53rd Street, New York, NY 10022. Entries must be received no later than February 28, 2005. Enter as often as you wish, but each entry must be mailed separately. One entry per envelope. Partially completed, illegible, or mechanically reproduced entries will not be accepted. Sponsor are not responsible for lost, late, mutilated, illegible, stolen, postage due, incomplete or misdirected entries. All entries become the property of Dualstar Entertainment Group, LLC, and will not be returned.

3. **Eligibility.** Sweepstakes open to all legal residents of the United States (excluding Colorado and Rhode Island) who are between the ages of five and fifteen on February 28, 2005 excluding employees and immediate family members of HarperCollins Publishers, Inc., ("HarperCollins"), Parachute Properties and Parachute Press, Inc., and their respective subsidiaries and affiliates, officers, directors, shareholders, employees, agents, attorneys, and other representatives and their immediate families (individually and collectively, "Parachute"), Dualstar Entertainment Group, LLC, and its subsidiaries and affiliates, officers, directors, shareholders, employees, agents, attorneys, and other representatives and their immediate families (individually and collectively, "Dualstar"), and their respective parent companies, affiliates, subsidiaries, advertising, promotion and fulfillment agencies, and the persons with whom each of the above are domiciled. All applicable federal, state and local laws and regulations apply. Offer void where prohibited or restricted by law.

4. **Odds of Winning.** Odds of winning depend on the total number of entries received. Approximately 300,000 sweepstakes announcements published. All prizes will be awarded. Winner will be randomly drawn on or about March 15, 2005, by HarperCollins, whose decision is final. Potential winner will be notified by mail and will be required to sign and return an affidavit of eligibility and release of liability within 14 days of notification. Prizes won by minors will be awarded to parent or legal guardian who must sign and return all required legal documents. By acceptance of their prize, winners consent to the use of their names, photographs, likeness, and biographical information by HarperCollins, Parachute, Dualstar, and for publicity purposes without further compensation except where prohibited.

5. **Grand Prize.** One Grand Prize Winner will win an Apple iPod®. Approximate retail value of prize totals $500.00.

6. **Prize Limitations.** All prizes will be awarded. Only one prize will be awarded per individual, family, or household. Prizes are nontransferable and cannot be sold or redeemed for cash. No cash substitute is available. Any federal, state, or local taxes are the responsibility of the winner. Sponsor may substitute prize of equal or greater value, if necessary, due to availability.

7. **Additional terms:** By participating, entrants agree a) to the official rules and decisions of the judges, which will be final in all respects; and to waive any claim to ambiguity of the official rules and b) to release, discharge, and hold harmless HarperCollins, Parachute, Dualstar, and their respective parent companies, affiliates, subsidiaries, employees and representatives and advertising, promotion and fulfillment agencies from and against any and all liability or damages associated with acceptance, use, or misuse of any prize received or participation in any Sweepstakes-related activity or participation in this Sweepstakes.

8. **Dispute Resolution.** Any dispute arising from this Sweepstakes will be determined according to the laws of the State of New York, without reference to its conflict of law principles, and the entrants consent to the personal jurisdiction of the State and Federal courts located in New York County and agree that such courts have exclusive jurisdiction over all such disputes.

9. **Winner Information.** To obtain the name of the winner, please send your request and a self-addressed stamped envelope (residents of Vermont may omit return postage) to New Adventures Apple iPod® Sweepstakes Winner, c/o HarperEntertainment, 10 East 53rd Street, New York, NY 10022 after April 15, 2005, but no later than October 15, 2005.

10. **Sweepstakes Sponsor.** HarperCollins Publishers, Inc. Apple© Corporation is not affiliated, connected or associated with this Sweepstakes in any manner and bears no responsibility for the administration of this Sweepstakes.

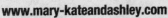